The Time-Traveling Kids

The Clockmaker's Secret

Jason Warren Bland

This is a work of fiction. Similarities to real people, places, or events are entirely coincidental.

THE CLOCKMAKER'S SECRET

First edition. November 12, 2024.

Copyright © 2024 Jason Bland.

Written by Jason Bland.

CHAPTER 1

THE DISCOVERY

It was the start of summer vacation, and the town of Willowbrook was buzzing with activity. The air was warm, carrying the scent of blooming flowers and freshly cut grass. Liam, Emma, and Zoe were strolling down Main Street, discussing what they'd do over the break. "Another summer with nothing exciting to do," Liam sighed, kicking a pebble along the sidewalk. "Oh, come on! We'll find something," Zoe replied optimistically, her eyes sparkling with the thrill of potential adventure.

As they passed the old clockmaker's shop, something caught Emma's attention. The door was slightly ajar, creaking open with a mysterious invitation. "Have you ever noticed this place?" Emma asked, pointing at the shop. "It looks... ancient." The shop hadn't changed since they were kids. It was a small, dusty building with a sign that read, "Thaddeus Tick's Clocks and Curiosities." Inside, the clocks ticked softly, their rhythmic sound filling the air with a sense of timelessness.

Liam peeked inside, curiosity getting the best of him. "I've heard old Mr. Tick never lets anyone in here. But look, the door's open..." Zoe, always the bold one, nudged them forward. "Let's go in! Maybe we'll find something interesting." The trio stepped inside, the smell of aged wood and metal filling their noses. Everywhere they looked, clocks of all shapes and sizes covered the walls, ticking in perfect harmony. At the far end of the room stood a tall, ornate grandfather clock with a shimmering, golden face. But it wasn't the clocks that caught their attention. In the corner of the room, hidden behind a thick curtain, was a door they'd never noticed before.

"Do you think we should go in?" Liam whispered, glancing around to make sure they were alone. Emma hesitated, but Zoe was already pulling the curtain aside, revealing a narrow staircase leading up to a dusty attic. "Only one way to find out!" Zoe grinned, heading up the stairs. Liam and Emma followed, their hearts pounding with excitement and just a hint of fear. At the top of the stairs, they entered a small, dimly lit attic filled with strange objects—ancient maps, mysterious trinkets, and boxes of old books.

But in the center of the room sat the strangest item of all: a small, brass device covered in strange symbols. Emma knelt beside it, running her fingers over the intricate carvings. "This looks like… some kind of clock. But I've never seen one like this before." Zoe picked it up carefully.

"Do you think it still works?" As if in response, the device began to hum softly. The hands on its tiny face spun faster and faster, and a warm glow filled the attic. Liam took a step back, his eyes wide. "Uh… guys? I think we just turned it on."

Before they could react, the world around them shifted, colors swirling and blending until everything went dark.

CHAPTER 2

THE MYSTERY OF THE DEVICE

Liam blinked, trying to clear his vision. The swirling colors had stopped, but they weren't in the attic anymore. Instead, they were standing in a field, with tall grass stretching out toward a small village in the distance.

"Where… are we?" Emma whispered, clutching the brass device in her hands. Zoe squinted at the scene before them. "This doesn't look like Willowbrook. It doesn't even look like our time. Look!" She pointed to a group of villagers in long, woolen tunics and cloaks, carrying baskets and tools. Emma's eyes widened as she took in the details.

The buildings were made of stone and wood, with thatched roofs and smoke curling up from small chimneys. Chickens clucked around the cobblestone streets, and a horse-drawn cart rumbled by. "I think… we've gone back in time," Liam said, his voice a mix of awe and disbelief. "This device… it's a time machine!" The trio looked down at the brass device, now silent in Emma's hands. Its face was no longer glowing, and the hands had returned to their original positions, as if waiting for another command.

"But… how?" Emma stammered. "How did it bring us here?" Zoe, ever the adventurer, grinned. "Who cares? This is amazing! We're in medieval times! We could see knights and castles and maybe even a dragon!" "Zoe, this isn't a game," Liam whispered urgently. "What if we can't get back?" Emma examined the device, trying to remember exactly how she'd touched it. "It was the center button, right? The one with the star symbol?" Zoe nodded.

"Yeah, but it's not glowing anymore. Maybe it needs time to… recharge?" The thought made them all uneasy. They were stuck here, in a time centuries before their own, with no way of knowing how to return home. Still, curiosity got the best of them, and they decided to explore. The village was bustling with activity as they walked through it, trying not to stand out. The villagers barely glanced at them, more concerned with their daily chores. Liam stopped by a cart piled with bread and cheese. "Look at this! Everything is handmade. No stores, no packaging…" A stern-looking woman with a basket of apples passed by and gave them a suspicious glance.

"Who are you children? Where are your families?" Thinking quickly, Emma replied, "We're travelers from a faraway village. Just… passing through." The woman raised an eyebrow but seemed satisfied and went on her way. They continued down the cobbled streets, taking in the sights and sounds. A group of children ran by, laughing and playing a game with wooden sticks, while an old man mended a leather boot by the side of the road.

Everything was so different, yet fascinating. But as they rounded a corner, they came face-to-face with a tall man in a dark cloak, his eyes sharp and watchful. He carried a small hammer at his side and wore a long chain with a small, ticking watch attached. "Who are you three?" he asked in a low voice, his gaze shifting between them.

"You don't look like you belong here." Emma held her breath, clutching the device tighter. "We… we're just travelers, sir." The man narrowed his eyes, but then he smiled, though it didn't reach his eyes. "Travelers, are you? Well, if it's time you're interested in, you should come with me. I know things about time that might… intrigue you." The friends exchanged nervous glances, but something about the man's words and the strange glint in his eye made them curious.

Without a word, they nodded, deciding to follow him. He led them down a narrow alley to a small, shadowed workshop filled with old clocks and tools. The ticking of gears and cogs filled the room, and the scent of oil and metal lingered in the air.

The man motioned for them to sit. "I am called Thaddeus, the clockmaker," he said, eyeing them closely. "And I know you didn't come here by accident." Emma's heart skipped a beat. "You... you know about the device?" Thaddeus nodded slowly, his eyes gleaming with knowledge.

"That device has been missing for centuries. And now, here it is... in the hands of three young travelers. You've got quite the journey ahead of you, my friends. But first, there's something you must learn." He leaned closer, his voice barely a whisper. "Time is a powerful force, but it demands respect.

If you wish to find your way back, you'll have to prove you're worthy of it." The friends sat in stunned silence, their minds racing with questions. What did Thaddeus mean? And what challenge would they have to face to return home?

CHAPTER 3

A GLIMPSE OF MEDIEVAL TIMES

Thaddeus watched them carefully, his fingers tapping rhythmically against his workbench. "You'll need to blend in if you want to survive here," he said, glancing at their modern clothes. "People in this town aren't used to strangers." Liam, Emma, and Zoe exchanged worried glances.

They hadn't thought much about how out of place they looked. The villagers had already been eyeing them with suspicion, and now they understood why. Thaddeus pulled a dusty chest from under his workbench and opened it. Inside were old, worn clothes: tunics, cloaks, and leather shoes.

"Put these on," he instructed, gesturing to the chest. "If you look like everyone else, you'll attract less attention." Emma pulled out a simple woolen dress, a bit faded but surprisingly comfortable, while Zoe found a green tunic and belt. Liam grabbed a brown tunic and a cloak that was just a little too big for him.

As they changed into their new outfits, Thaddeus continued, "You must also learn to act the part. In this time, people's lives are simpler but harder. Be mindful of their ways, their customs. Respect is earned here, not given." "Thank you for helping us," Emma said, grateful. "But why are you doing this?" Thaddeus looked at her, a strange sadness in his eyes.

"Let's just say I have a… special interest in travelers like you." His cryptic answer only deepened the mystery, but before they could press him for more, Thaddeus handed them each a piece of dark bread. "Eat up. You'll need your strength if you're to understand this place."

They ate quietly, taking in their surroundings. The clockmaker's workshop was filled with peculiar objects:

gears of all sizes, unfinished clocks, tiny glass vials of oils and dyes, and several sheets of parchment filled with complicated diagrams. It felt like a hidden world, buzzing with secrets. After they finished, Thaddeus gave them one last warning. "Stay close to the village.

The woods and hills can be dangerous, especially for strangers like yourselves." With that, the friends ventured outside, trying to look as though they belonged. They walked through the village square, now bustling with activity. A blacksmith hammered away at a sword, his muscles rippling with each strike, while a group of women gathered at a well, chatting and laughing as they drew water. A boy about their age waved at them, his face streaked with dirt. "New here, aren't ya?"

Liam nodded, doing his best to seem casual. "Just… passing through." The boy grinned. "I'm Tom. You look like you could use a guide. Want me to show you around?" Emma was about to decline, but Zoe quickly jumped in. "Yes, please! We'd love that." Tom led them through the winding streets, explaining things with an enthusiasm that made everything feel exciting. "That's the baker," he said, pointing to a shop with a sweet, yeasty aroma drifting out. "Best bread in the village. And over there's the tannery—smells bad, but that's where we get leather for our boots and belts." As they explored, the friends tried to take in as much as they could about this strange world.

Everything was different—the clothes, the buildings, even the language sounded a bit unusual, though they could understand it well enough. But as they passed the stone walls of the village church, a group of men wearing cloaks and carrying long staffs stopped to stare at them. One of the men narrowed his eyes, as though he recognized something off about their presence.

Emma whispered to Liam, "We need to be careful. People are already watching us." Liam nodded. "If we stick with Tom, maybe we won't stand out as much." They continued on, taking mental notes and learning as much as they could. The sun was beginning to set, casting a golden glow over the village, when Tom brought them to a clearing near the village edge. A sturdy wooden bridge crossed a rushing stream, and beyond it, the dense forest loomed. "There's the forest," Tom said, lowering his voice. "It's dangerous, but some say the clockmaker goes there sometimes. People say he's… different." "Different?" Zoe asked, intrigued. "Yeah," Tom replied.

"Some think he has powers or knows things no one else does. That's why folks don't go near him unless they really need to." Emma shivered, glancing back toward the village. "We should head back. Thaddeus warned us to stay close to the village." But as they turned to leave, Zoe spotted something lying near the bridge—a small, rusted key with strange symbols etched into it. She picked it up, studying it closely. "Guys," she whispered, showing them the key. "Do you think this could be part of… his secret?" The friends exchanged a look, knowing they were in deeper than they'd imagined. With one last glance at the forest, they headed back to the village, holding the mysterious key tightly.

CHAPTER 4

FITTING IN

The next morning, Liam, Emma, and Zoe woke up in a small, cozy room above Thaddeus's workshop. Sunlight streamed through a tiny window, casting warm patterns on the wooden floor.

They stretched and looked around, noticing simple furnishings, a sturdy wooden table, a few chairs, and beds with woolen blankets. "We need to act like we belong here," Emma whispered, remembering Thaddeus's advice from the previous day.

Zoe nodded, glancing at her tunic to ensure it looked natural. "Let's start by blending in. Maybe we can help around the workshop or the village to earn some trust." Liam, always the practical one, agreed. "Good idea. Let's see what we can do without drawing too much attention." As they descended the stairs, the workshop buzzed with activity. Thaddeus was hunched over a workbench, carefully repairing a pocket watch.

The rhythmic ticking of clocks filled the air, creating a comforting, familiar sound despite the unfamiliar surroundings. "Good morning," Thaddeus greeted them without looking up. "I trust you slept well." "Morning, Mr. Tick," Emma replied politely. "Is there anything we can help with today?" Thaddeus glanced up, a hint of a smile playing on his lips. "Actually, yes. We could use some assistance organizing these parts. It's much easier with extra hands."

The friends nodded eagerly and set to work, sorting gears, springs, and tiny screws into labeled boxes. As they worked, Thaddeus shared stories about clockmaking and the history of the village. "You see," he explained, "clocks are more than just timekeepers here. They represent the passage of life, the cycles of nature, and the importance of every moment." Liam found himself fascinated by the intricate mechanisms, while Zoe enjoyed the teamwork. Emma, always observant, kept an eye on the mysterious key they had found by the bridge, pondering its significance.

After a few hours, Thaddeus called them over. "You've done well today. As a token of appreciation, I have something for each of you." He handed them small, handcrafted items, Emma received a leather pouch, Zoe got a sturdy wristband, and Liam was given a miniature compass. "These might come in handy on your journey," Thaddeus said with a knowing look.

"Thank you, Mr. Tick," Zoe said, slipping the wristband onto her arm. As the day went on, the friends began to feel more comfortable in their roles. They helped mend clocks, deliver messages around the village, and even learned a few local phrases from Tom, who visited to check on their progress. Later that afternoon, Tom returned, excitement evident in his eyes.

"Hey, I found something interesting by the old mill," he said, beckoning them to follow. Curious, the trio followed Tom through the winding village streets to the outskirts where the old mill stood. The structure was weathered, with vines creeping up its stone walls and the sound of the nearby stream filling the silence. "There's a hidden compartment here," Tom explained, pointing to a loose stone in the wall. "I've been trying to open it for weeks."

Emma stepped forward, holding the mysterious key they had found. "Maybe this can help." Tom handed her the key, and with a bit of effort, the compartment sprang open, revealing a small, dusty box inside. Emma carefully lifted the lid, revealing an assortment of old papers, a faded map, and a strange, shimmering pendant.

"What is this?" Liam asked, peering over her shoulder. Thaddeus appeared beside them, his expression serious. "Ah, you've found one of the clockmaker's secrets. That pendant is no ordinary trinket,l it's a key to unlocking deeper mysteries of time itself." Zoe's eyes sparkled with excitement. "What does it do?" Thaddeus smiled mysteriously. "That, my friends, is something you'll discover as your journey continues.

For now, keep it safe and remember that every discovery leads to another piece of the puzzle."

As the sun began to set, casting long shadows over the village, the friends returned to their room, the pendant safely tucked away. They sat together, reflecting on the day's events. "I feel like we're really starting to fit in," Liam said, looking around the room. "Yeah," Emma agreed.

"But there's still so much we don't know. What do you think Thaddeus meant by proving we're worthy of controlling the time device?" Zoe held up the pendant, its surface shimmering in the evening light. "Whatever it is, I think this pendant is going to be a big part of it. We need to figure out what it does."

As they pondered their next steps, the brass time device on the table began to glow faintly, the symbols on its surface shimmering with a soft light. The friends exchanged uneasy glances, wondering if their adventures were only just beginning.

Chapter 5

Meeting The Clockmaker

The following morning, Liam, Emma, and Zoe found Thaddeus in his workshop, deeply focused on a delicate timepiece. The morning light filtered through the small window, illuminating the intricate mechanisms on his workbench.

The rhythmic ticking of clocks filled the room, lending a sense of calm as they prepared to speak with him. Emma approached first, holding the shimmering pendant they'd discovered in the hidden compartment. "Mr. Tick, we found this near the old mill yesterday. You said it was important." Thaddeus looked up, his expression softening as he examined the pendant. "Ah, yes. You've found an ancient key, one that opens more than just doors." Liam tilted his head, intrigued.

"What do you mean?" The clockmaker gestured for them to sit around the workbench. His gaze grew distant, as though he was looking back in time. "That pendant was created by the very first timekeepers, those who knew how to move between worlds, much like you."

The friends exchanged a glance. "Timekeepers?" Zoe repeated. "You mean... like time travelers?" Thaddeus nodded. "Yes. But they weren't ordinary travelers. They had an understanding of time's delicate balance. They could only move through time when absolutely necessary, to preserve or protect certain events." He looked at them, a hint of pride in his gaze. "It seems you have been chosen to carry on their legacy." Emma, clutching the pendant, felt a sense of awe mixed with responsibility.

"What are we supposed to do with it?" "The pendant," Thaddeus explained, "is a map. It will guide you to where you need to go, but only if you're ready for the journey. Time has a way of testing those who try to master it." Liam's eyes widened. "So, if we use the pendant with the time device... it could take us somewhere specific?" Thaddeus nodded.

"Precisely. But there's one thing you must understand: each journey will come with a task. Something you'll need to complete before you can return." Zoe looked down at the brass time device on the table, the glowing symbols on its surface casting a warm light. "Is this why we were brought to the medieval village?" "Yes," Thaddeus replied, his tone grave.

"Time has a way of drawing people to the places they're needed most. But be cautious. Time can be unforgiving to those who meddle with its flow." As they absorbed his words, Emma's mind raced with possibilities. She looked at Thaddeus, curiosity burning in her eyes. "So, what task do we have here?"

The clockmaker took a deep breath, considering her question. "In this time, there is a rift, a small imbalance that needs to be corrected. The village is in danger of losing an essential part of its history, something that will change the future in ways we can't predict. You must find this imbalance and set it right." The friends exchanged glances, excitement mixed with trepidation.

They didn't fully understand what Thaddeus meant, but they knew they had to try. "What should we look for?" Liam asked, his voice determined. Thaddeus leaned in, lowering his voice. "There is an artifact hidden in the village, an ancient sundial that holds powerful knowledge. It was placed here centuries ago by one of the original timekeepers. But now, someone is looking to take it, someone who would use it for dark purposes." Emma's heart quickened.

"Do you know who it is?" The clockmaker shook his head. "Not yet. But the pendant will guide you. It will glow when you're near the sundial. Follow it, and it will lead you to the artifact before it's too late." With a steady hand, Thaddeus pointed to the pendant's central stone. "Hold it up to the light, and you'll see." Emma lifted the pendant, and as the morning sunlight struck it, the pendant glowed softly, casting a warm, golden light.

Tiny symbols appeared on its surface, forming what looked like a miniature map. Zoe gasped, her eyes wide with wonder. "It's pointing to… the forest, near the clearing." "Then that's where we start," Liam said, a sense of resolve in his voice. "We'll find the sundial and protect it from whoever wants to steal it."

Thaddeus placed a hand on Liam's shoulder, his face solemn. "Be cautious, my friends. The forest holds secrets, and those who seek the sundial will stop at nothing to possess it. Trust each other, and trust the pendant. It will guide you." The friends nodded, each of them feeling the weight of their mission.

They had come to this time and place for a reason, and they were determined to see it through. As they left the workshop, pendant in hand and hearts pounding, the excitement of adventure mixed with a new sense of purpose.

They knew the journey ahead would be dangerous, but with the clockmaker's wisdom and the pendant's guidance, they were ready to face whatever lay in the forest's shadows.

CHAPTER 6

INTO THE WOODS

The sun was high in the sky as Liam, Emma, and Zoe made their way toward the forest's edge, the pendant glowing faintly in Emma's hand. A light breeze rustled the trees, and the air felt thick with anticipation.

They knew they were stepping into unknown territory. "This place feels different," Zoe murmured as they crossed the old wooden bridge. "Like it's hiding something." Liam, always cautious, glanced around. "We need to stay alert. Thaddeus warned us that the forest isn't safe." Emma held the pendant up to check the glowing symbols.

The map seemed to shift as they moved, the pendant's light flickering and guiding them deeper into the woods. Shadows danced around them as they navigated a narrow path covered in moss and tangled roots. After a while, they came upon a clearing, and in its center stood a cluster of large stones arranged in a circle. The pendant's glow brightened as they drew closer. "This has to be it," Emma whispered, her heart racing.

Liam and Zoe moved to examine the stones. Each one was etched with strange markings similar to the symbols on the pendant. But there was no sundial, just these ancient stones standing silently under the canopy of trees. "Where's the sundial?" Zoe asked, scanning the area. Just then, they heard a faint crackling sound, like dry leaves crunching underfoot. Liam froze, signaling for the others to stay still. They huddled together, listening. The footsteps grew louder, slow and deliberate. Someone was coming their way. Emma held her breath, gripping the pendant tightly.

Through the trees, they caught sight of a shadowy figure moving with purpose. The figure wore a dark cloak, and although they couldn't see his face, there was something menacing about his presence. "Let's hide," Liam whispered. The friends ducked behind one of the larger stones, peeking out just enough to watch the figure approach. He moved into the clearing, stopping right where they'd been moments before. For a moment, he simply stood there, his head turning as if searching for something.

The figure pulled a small object from his cloak, a dagger with a gleaming silver blade. He held it up, pointing it toward the stones as though testing something. Emma stifled a gasp. The dagger had symbols etched along its blade, similar to those on the stones and the pendant. Whoever this man was, he clearly knew about the sundial and the ancient markings. "Do you think he's looking for the same thing we are?" Zoe whispered, her voice barely audible. Liam nodded. "Definitely. And I don't think he's here to protect it." The man muttered something under his breath, words they couldn't make out.

Then, to their horror, he lifted the dagger and struck it against one of the stones. A strange sound echoed through the clearing, and the symbols on the stone began to glow, casting an eerie blue light. The friends exchanged alarmed glances. Whatever he was doing, it was awakening something within the stones. "We have to stop him," Emma whispered, her voice filled with urgency. Liam shook his head. "Not yet. We don't know what we're dealing with." But before they could decide on a plan, the man lowered the dagger, seemingly satisfied.

He pocketed the blade and turned to leave, disappearing back into the forest. The friends stayed hidden until they were sure he was gone, each of them tense and on high alert. "What was he doing?" Zoe asked as they emerged from behind the stone. "I think he was testing something," Emma replied, inspecting the glowing symbols. "It's almost as if he activated the stones." Liam frowned, examining the markings. "Maybe the sundial is hidden somehow. What if it only appears when the stones are activated?"

Emma held up the pendant, letting its light shine on the stones. Slowly, the glow of the symbols grew stronger, and in the center of the stone circle, the ground began to shift. With a soft rumbling, an ancient sundial rose from beneath the earth. Its stone surface was smooth, and intricate carvings adorned its edges. At its center was a pointed needle that cast a long shadow, despite the trees around them.

The friends stared in awe. They had found it, the sundial Thaddeus had told them about. Zoe reached out, touching the sundial's cool surface. "It's beautiful." Emma, still holding the pendant, felt a surge of energy pulse through her. "This must be the artifact we're supposed to protect." But Liam's expression was serious. "If that man comes back, he'll try to take it." "We can't let him," Emma said, her eyes determined. "This sundial holds too much power. If it falls into the wrong hands..." They gathered around the sundial, examining its carvings.

Along its base, they noticed a row of symbols matching those on the pendant. "Maybe these symbols are a code," Zoe suggested, tracing her fingers over the carvings. "Or a way to unlock its full power." Liam nodded. "Thaddeus mentioned that time is fragile. I think this sundial can change things, maybe even allow someone to travel to different points in history." Emma shivered, realizing the weight of their discovery.

"We need to tell Thaddeus about the man we saw. He might know who he is and how to stop him." As they prepared to leave the clearing, a soft hum filled the air, emanating from the sundial.

The pendant in Emma's hand glowed once more, and they felt the world around them shift ever so slightly, as if the forest itself was aware of their presence. "We need to hurry," Liam said, leading them back toward the village. "If that man realizes we found the sundial, he'll be back." With one last look at the ancient sundial, the friends sprinted through the forest, their minds racing.

They now knew that their journey was more dangerous than they'd ever imagined. And with a mysterious stranger also seeking the sundial, they realized they weren't the only ones drawn into the secrets of time.

CHAPTER 7

UNCOVERING SECRETS

Breathless and tense, Liam, Emma, and Zoe made their way back to Thaddeus's workshop. The pendant had stopped glowing, but its warm weight in Emma's hand reminded her of the incredible and dangerous discovery they'd made in the forest.

Thaddeus looked up from his workbench as they burst in, his eyes widening slightly when he saw their expressions. "Back so soon, are you? Did you find what you were looking for?" Emma held out the pendant, her voice urgent. "We found the sundial, Mr. Tick. Just like you said. But we weren't the only ones." Thaddeus's gaze sharpened. "Someone else was there?" Liam nodded, his voice low. "A man in a cloak.

He had a dagger with symbols on it, like the ones on the stones and the sundial. He... did something to the stones, and it made them glow." Thaddeus's face grew serious. "That means he's found a way to activate the sundial. If he succeeds in using it, the balance of time could be severely disturbed."

Emma frowned, remembering the man's focused intensity. "Who is he?" Thaddeus sighed, looking away as if searching for the right words. "His name is Balthazar. He's a relic hunter—a seeker of ancient, powerful artifacts. But he cares only for the power they grant him, not the balance they're meant to preserve." "Why would he want the sundial?" Zoe asked, glancing at the pendant in Emma's hand. "The sundial isn't just a piece of history," Thaddeus explained, his voice grave. "It holds the knowledge of past and future timekeepers. It can be used to travel to any point in time, but only when paired with the right key." He gestured to the pendant. "And that's why he's after it.

With the sundial and the key together, he could access powerful secrets—and even rewrite history." The friends exchanged worried glances. The stakes had suddenly become very real. "What do we do?" Liam asked, determination in his voice. "We can't let him have it." Thaddeus nodded. "Precisely. Balthazar doesn't know that you hold the key, which gives us a slight advantage. But we must act quickly." He reached into a drawer and pulled out a small, dusty book with a worn leather cover.

The title was faint but read Chronicles of the Timekeepers. Thaddeus placed it on the table and flipped through the pages, stopping at a hand-drawn map. "This book details some of the protections placed around the sundial," he explained, showing them the map. "Long ago, timekeepers left clues to ensure that only those with pure intentions could unlock its full power."

Emma studied the map, her finger tracing a line from the village to a marked point labeled "Guardian's Peak." "This must be the place," she whispered. "The book says it's where the original timekeepers left a message." Thaddeus nodded. "Yes. The message will reveal how to safeguard the sundial. If we can reach Guardian's Peak before Balthazar, we might learn how to secure the sundial so he can't misuse it." Zoe glanced nervously toward the door. "What if he follows us? He seemed pretty determined." "We'll have to be careful," Liam said, his voice steady. "But we can't let him get his hands on this power."

Thaddeus's gaze softened as he looked at them. "I wish I could join you, but the village needs me. Besides, the journey to Guardian's Peak is one you must make on your own. It's the true test of a timekeeper." He handed Emma a small leather pouch filled with herbs. "For energy and strength," he explained. "The path to the Peak is steep and treacherous, and the air grows thin as you climb. You'll need all the strength you can muster."

Emma accepted the pouch gratefully. "Thank you, Mr. Tick. We'll make sure Balthazar doesn't get what he wants." With a final nod from Thaddeus, the friends gathered their supplies, hearts pounding with a mixture of fear and excitement. Guardian's Peak lay just beyond the forest, shrouded in mist and mystery. They knew the climb would be difficult, but they were ready to face whatever challenges lay ahead. As they made their way out of the village, the pendant in Emma's hand pulsed with a faint warmth, guiding them once more.

They followed the narrow path into the forest, heading toward the towering silhouette of Guardian's Peak in the distance. After a while, they reached the base of the mountain. The path was rocky and steep, with roots and vines twisting along the ground like obstacles designed to trip them. They climbed in silence, focusing on their steps as the forest canopy grew denser around them. Finally, they reached a plateau with a clear view of the valley below.

The village looked tiny, nestled among the trees, and the air felt still and sacred. At the center of the plateau stood a stone marker, ancient and covered in moss. Carved into its surface was a symbol—the same one that adorned the pendant. "This is it," Zoe whispered, touching the symbol. "This must be the place where the message is hidden." As Emma held the pendant up to the stone, the symbols on both began to glow.

A soft hum filled the air, and words appeared on the stone, written in the same ancient script they'd seen on the sundial: "Only those who walk the path of time with pure hearts may hold its secrets." The friends exchanged glances, feeling the weight of the message. "What does it mean?" Liam asked, his voice barely above a whisper.

Thaddeus's words echoed in Emma's mind: Time tests those who seek to control it. She looked down at the pendant, feeling its warmth pulse in her hand. "I think it means that only those who respect time, who aren't seeking power, can truly use it." Zoe nodded slowly. "If we're here to protect the sundial, it means we're worthy of its secrets.

But if Balthazar tries to use it… maybe the sundial will resist him." Liam's face lit up with understanding. "So we just need to keep the pendant safe, and the sundial's power will remain protected." As they stood in silent agreement, a distant rustling caught their attention. They turned to see a shadow moving through the trees below, Balthazar was approaching, his cloak billowing as he climbed the mountain path toward them.

Emma gripped the pendant tightly, feeling a surge of courage. "He's coming. We need to go, now!" The friends quickly moved away from the plateau, slipping back onto the winding path that led down the other side of Guardian's Peak. They kept low, their footsteps silent as they navigated the steep terrain.

As they descended, Emma glanced back to see Balthazar reach the plateau. He stared at the stone marker, his face twisted in frustration as he realized the friends were one step ahead of him. "We'll be ready for him," Liam whispered, determination etched on his face.

With renewed resolve, they made their way back toward the village, hearts pounding with the knowledge that they were now the true protectors of the sundial. The power to shape history lay within their hands, and they were ready to defend it.

CHAPTER 8

THE VILLAGE DEFENDERS

Back in the village, the friends gathered in Thaddeus's workshop, their minds buzzing with everything they had learned. Outside, the sun was dipping below the horizon, casting long shadows over the cobblestone streets.

They knew Balthazar would be planning his next move, and they had to be ready. Thaddeus, who had been deep in thought since their return, finally spoke up. "If Balthazar realizes you have the pendant, he'll stop at nothing to take it.

We must find a way to protect the sundial and keep him from entering the forest." "But how?" Zoe asked, glancing around the workshop. "He seems to know every trick in the book." Liam stepped forward, his face serious. "What if we set up some defenses around the village? Traps, maybe, or some way to delay him if he tries to enter the forest." Emma's eyes brightened. "That could work! If we create obstacles, he'll have a harder time reaching the sundial and we can buy ourselves enough time to come up with a plan."

Thaddeus nodded thoughtfully, pacing the workshop. "It's a good idea. I have a few things here that might help. Tools, ropes... even a few ancient wards I've collected over the years." He reached up to a shelf, pulling down a small, weathered box. Inside were several vials filled with a shimmering blue powder, each labeled in an old, spidery script. "These are protection powders," he explained, showing them the vials.

"Sprinkle them along the path, and anyone with ill intentions will find it difficult to pass." The friends eagerly took the vials, dividing them among themselves. "We'll line the main path from the village to the sundial," Emma said. "And maybe set up a few distractions along the way to throw him off."

Thaddeus's eyes sparkled with approval. "Smart thinking. And I have one more thing that might be of use." He turned to a large chest in the corner of the workshop, opening it to reveal an intricately carved horn. Its surface was etched with symbols that glowed faintly in the dim light.

"This horn was once used by the guardians of the sundial," Thaddeus explained. "In times of danger, it can summon allies to your side. But it must be used wisely, the sound carries far, and it may attract more than just friends." Emma took the horn carefully, feeling the weight of its ancient power. "Thank you, Mr. Tick. We'll only use it if we absolutely have to." With their plan in place, the friends left the workshop and set out into the village, each of them feeling a renewed sense of purpose. They worked quickly, placing the vials along the path and setting up makeshift barriers wherever they could.

Liam found a bundle of thorny vines and laid them across one of the narrower trails, while Zoe gathered fallen branches to create a barrier around the forest's edge. As they worked, the villagers watched from their doorways, some of them whispering anxiously. Word had spread of the mysterious stranger in the cloak, and many of the villagers sensed that something unusual was happening. Finally, as darkness settled over the village, the friends gathered near the entrance to the forest.

The night was quiet, and a sense of anticipation hung in the air. They knew Balthazar would come eventually, and they were ready to face him. An hour passed, then another. The village lay still, and the only sounds were the distant hoots of owls and the soft rustling of leaves in the breeze. But just as they began to relax, a faint glimmer of movement caught their attention at the edge of the forest.

There, emerging from the shadows, was Balthazar. His dark cloak blended with the night, but his dagger gleamed as he held it up, inspecting the path before him. The friends crouched low, watching as he took a few cautious steps forward. Balthazar paused, sniffing the air as if sensing something was amiss. He stepped closer, his gaze scanning the path where the protection powders had been sprinkled. The vials' magic began to glow faintly, creating an invisible barrier that stopped him in his tracks. "What trickery is this?" he muttered, raising his dagger.

Emma's heart pounded as she watched him struggle against the invisible wall. She clutched the pendant tightly, feeling its warmth pulse in her hand. It was as if the artifact itself was lending them strength. Balthazar took a step back, frustration etched on his face. But instead of retreating, he turned and circled around the barrier, looking for another way in. "He's going to find a way through," Zoe whispered urgently. "We have to do something."

Emma nodded, her hand still on the ancient horn Thaddeus had given her. "We might need to call for help. But are we ready for what it might summon?" Liam gave her a reassuring nod. "Whatever it takes, Emma. We can't let him reach the sundial." Taking a deep breath, Emma lifted the horn to her lips and blew a long, low note that echoed through the forest. The sound seemed to travel for miles, filling the night with its eerie, powerful call.

For a moment, there was silence. But then, faintly at first, the sound of footsteps and rustling leaves grew louder. Figures emerged from the shadows, villagers carrying torches, their faces set with determination. They had answered the call, ready to defend their home. Balthazar's eyes widened as he saw the crowd gathering around him.

He backed away, his dagger raised defensively. "Stay back!" he snarled. "You don't know what you're meddling with!" But the villagers didn't falter. Led by Thaddeus, they formed a protective line between Balthazar and the path to the sundial.

"This is our village," Thaddeus said firmly, his voice carrying through the darkness. "And we won't let you disturb the peace we've kept for generations." Balthazar sneered, clutching his dagger tightly. "Fools. Do you really think you can stand against me?"

Just then, Emma felt the pendant grow warm once more, and the symbols on its surface glowed with a fierce light. She lifted it high, feeling its energy surge through her.

"You may have power, Balthazar," she said, her voice strong and steady. "But you don't have what matters most: the strength of the people who protect this place."

With that, she stepped forward, holding the pendant between them like a shield. The glow intensified, casting a radiant light that seemed to push Balthazar back. Balthazar took another step, his eyes narrowing as he realized he was outmatched.

With a snarl of frustration, he lowered his dagger and backed away into the shadows. "This isn't over," he hissed, his voice filled with malice. "The sundial will be mine. And when it is, you'll all regret standing in my way."

With one last glare, he disappeared into the darkness, leaving the village in a tense, uneasy silence. The friends and villagers watched as he vanished, each of them feeling a mixture of relief and apprehension. They knew he would be back, and that the struggle to protect the sundial was far from over. Thaddeus turned to Emma, Zoe, and Liam, his eyes filled with pride. "You did well," he said quietly. "But this is only the beginning.

The sundial's power has awakened, and others like Balthazar may come looking for it. We'll have to be vigilant." Emma nodded, feeling the weight of responsibility settle on her shoulders.

She glanced at her friends, knowing they felt it too. But despite the danger, they were ready to face whatever challenges lay ahead.

With the villagers by their side and the ancient artifacts in their care, they knew they had the strength to protect the sundial, and the secrets of time itself.

CHAPTER 9

THE KEEPER'S WARNING

The air was thick with tension as the villagers began to disperse after Balthazar's retreat. Despite the temporary victory, Emma, Liam, and Zoe felt the weight of the situation pressing down on them.

They gathered again in Thaddeus's workshop, determined to learn more about the sundial and how they could protect it. Thaddeus had lit candles around the room, casting flickering shadows on the walls.

He pulled out the Chronicles of the Timekeepers, carefully turning its delicate pages to reveal illustrations and stories about the guardians who had come before them. "Long ago," he began, his voice resonating with the gravity of the history they were about to uncover, "the sundial was entrusted to a group of timekeepers who understood its power. They formed a council that dedicated their lives to protecting the balance of time."

Emma leaned forward, her interest piqued. "What happened to them?" Thaddeus gestured to an illustration showing a grand gathering of people in flowing robes, standing around a magnificent sundial. "Over time, as the power of the sundial grew, so did the temptation of those who sought to misuse it.

The council was forced to take measures to safeguard the sundial, hiding its true location and creating layers of protection." Zoe traced a finger over the illustration. "But Balthazar seems to know more than he should. How can we outsmart him if he's already aware of the sundial's significance?"

Thaddeus turned to a page with sketches of various symbols. "These are the warnings left by the last council of timekeepers. They foresaw that those driven by greed would come for the sundial, and so they embedded clues within the symbols.

If you can decipher these warnings, it may help you understand what Balthazar truly seeks." Emma flipped through the pages, her eyes scanning the symbols that seemed to dance across the parchment. "What do they mean?" "Each symbol corresponds to a different aspect of time," Thaddeus explained. "The sun represents the past, the moon signifies the present, and the stars signify the future. If Balthazar is seeking the sundial's power, he must first solve the riddles associated with these symbols."

Liam's brow furrowed as he took in the information. "And if he can't solve them?" "Then he cannot access the sundial's full power," Thaddeus replied. "But be warned, he may use force or trickery to find a way around them.

This makes it imperative that you understand the riddles before he does." Emma felt a surge of determination. "We need to figure this out. If we can decipher these riddles, we can stay one step ahead of him."

The friends spent the next few hours poring over the Chronicles of the Timekeepers, searching for anything that might hint at the riddles Balthazar would face. They worked together, each contributing their thoughts and ideas, their voices growing more animated as they uncovered clues. Finally, they reached a page filled with intricate drawings of the sun, moon, and stars, accompanied by cryptic lines of text.

Emma read aloud: "To know the past, seek the light of the sun; In shadows cast, your journey has begun. In the present, the moon holds a secret key; Follow its path to set your fate free. And the stars will guide when the time is right, For in the night sky, the future shines bright."

"That's it!" Zoe exclaimed, her eyes shining with excitement. "These are the riddles! We need to break them down." Liam pointed to the first line. "The sun represents the past. Maybe we need to find a way to uncover something that's been hidden or forgotten." Thaddeus nodded, encouraging their exploration. "Yes, the sun's light could symbolize an event or a location.

Perhaps the first step is in the village itself. There are many tales from our past that may hold clues." "The moon," Zoe continued, "could be about finding something in the present, a location where the moon's light shines at a specific time.

And the stars might mean we have to wait for a certain event to happen before we can act." Emma felt a thrill of anticipation. "If we can interpret these correctly, we might be able to stay ahead of Balthazar. But we need to act quickly. He'll be back."

Thaddeus placed a hand on Emma's shoulder, his expression serious. "Remember, the riddles are not just about finding answers; they are tests of character. You must face challenges that will reveal your true intentions. Be prepared for anything." As the candles flickered in the dim light, the friends made a pact.

They would work together to decipher the riddles, pooling their skills and knowledge to protect the sundial from Balthazar's grasp. "We'll meet at dawn," Emma declared. "We'll start with the stories of the village and see what we can uncover about our past." The others nodded, and with a sense of purpose, they left the workshop.

Outside, the moon hung high in the sky, casting a silver glow over the village. Emma couldn't shake the feeling that they were being watched, but she pushed the thought aside.

As she walked home, her mind whirred with possibilities. What secrets did the village hold? What dangers awaited them? The next day would bring new challenges, but they would face them together.

With the pendant in her pocket and the riddles of the timekeepers before them, Emma felt a glimmer of hope. They were the guardians now, the defenders of time, and they would not let Balthazar win.

CHAPTER 10

INTO THE PAST

The first rays of dawn peeked through the curtains as Emma sprang from her bed, her heart racing with anticipation. Today was the day they would start solving the riddles.

She quickly dressed and rushed to meet Liam and Zoe at their chosen meeting place, the old oak tree in the village square. As she approached, she spotted her friends waiting, their faces illuminated by the morning sun.

Liam was flipping through the Chronicles of the Timekeepers, and Zoe was sketching ideas in her notebook. "Good morning!" Emma called out, her voice bright with excitement. "Ready to crack some riddles?" "Absolutely!" Zoe replied, her eyes sparkling. "I couldn't sleep a wink thinking about all the possibilities." Liam closed the book, a determined look on his face. "Let's start by exploring the village. Thaddeus mentioned that there are many stories tied to our past, and we might find clues in the places we visit."

With their plan in place, the trio set off into the village, eager to uncover the secrets hidden in its history. The streets were quiet, with only the sound of birds chirping in the trees. As they walked, Emma felt a sense of belonging; the village was their home, and now they were part of its story.

They decided to begin at the village's library, a quaint stone building adorned with ivy. Inside, the air was cool and filled with the scent of aged parchment. A friendly librarian greeted them, her glasses perched on her nose as she sorted through a pile of books.

"Good morning, children! What brings you here today?" she asked. Emma smiled. "We're looking for stories about the village's history. We believe there may be something hidden that relates to the sundial." The librarian's eyes twinkled with interest. "Ah, the sundial! A beautiful artifact with many tales. Follow me; I have just the thing." She led them to a section of the library dedicated to local history and began pulling books from the shelves.

"This one," she said, handing Emma an ancient tome, "contains stories of the village's founding and its protectors." As they flipped through the pages, Zoe pointed out an illustration of the sundial surrounded by villagers, their faces filled with joy. "Look at how they're gathered around it! It's like a festival." "Maybe the sundial was once a place of celebration," Liam suggested.

"A gathering point for important events." After poring over several books and finding snippets about festivals, ceremonies, and local legends, they stumbled upon a reference to a forgotten relic, the Heart of the Village. "It says here that the Heart of the Village is a stone that holds the memories of the community," Emma read aloud. "It's kept in a hidden cave nearby and is said to resonate with the energy of the sundial." "That could be what we're looking for!" Zoe exclaimed. "If we find the Heart, we might uncover more about the past and what Balthazar wants."

The librarian overheard them and chimed in. "Many villagers have searched for the Heart, but none have found it. They say it's protected by the spirits of the old timekeepers, and only those with pure intentions can access it."

Emma felt a mix of excitement and apprehension. "Then we have to find it. It could be our key to stopping Balthazar." After thanking the librarian for her help, they set off to locate the cave mentioned in the book. Following the descriptions, they made their way through the village and into the surrounding woods, the path winding deeper into the trees.

As they walked, Emma felt the pendant growing warm against her chest, almost as if it was guiding them. "This way!" she called, noticing a faint shimmer of light filtering through the leaves.

The deeper they ventured, the more they could feel a subtle shift in the atmosphere, a sense of magic hanging in the air.

Finally, they arrived at a rocky outcropping, and before them was the entrance to a cave, partially hidden by vines. "This must be it!" Liam said, his eyes wide with wonder. With cautious excitement, they stepped inside. The cave was cool and dark, and the walls sparkled with minerals that glinted like stars. They switched on their flashlights, illuminating the path ahead. As they ventured further, they encountered strange symbols carved into the rock, symbols that mirrored those in the Chronicles of the Timekeepers. Emma pointed them out, recognizing the sun, moon, and stars among the carvings.

"This is a good sign. We're on the right track." They followed the winding passage until they reached a larger chamber. In the center stood a pedestal, and atop it lay the Heart of the Village. The stone glowed softly, pulsing with a warm, inviting light. "This is incredible!" Zoe gasped, her voice echoing in the stillness of the cave. Emma stepped forward, feeling drawn to the stone. As she reached out to touch it, the air around them shimmered, and a gentle voice filled the chamber. "Only the true guardians may wield the Heart's power. Are you prepared to protect your village and its history?" Emma's heart raced. "We are! We'll do whatever it takes to keep our village safe." The light of the Heart brightened, illuminating the cave and revealing intricate carvings along the walls, images of the village's past and the timekeepers who had come before them.

Liam and Zoe stood beside her, their expressions filled with resolve. "We're in this together," Liam said, placing a hand on Emma's shoulder. "Let's unlock the secrets of the past." As they placed their hands on the Heart, a surge of energy coursed through them, filling the chamber with warmth and light. Visions flashed before their eyes, scenes of the village thriving, the sundial serving as a beacon of hope, and the timekeepers standing guard, protecting the balance of time.

Suddenly, the vision shifted, showing Balthazar looming over the sundial, his eyes filled with greed. Emma felt a jolt of fear, but alongside it was a newfound determination. They could not let this future come to pass. The light dimmed, and the Heart settled into a calm glow. They had seen the power it held, and they understood the weight of their responsibility.

They were the new guardians now, and they would defend their village at all costs. "We need to get back and prepare for Balthazar," Zoe said, breaking the spell. "We can use what we learned here to confront him." With the Heart's energy still resonating within them, the friends turned to leave the cave, filled with hope and purpose.

They had unlocked a part of the village's history, and now they were armed with the knowledge to protect it. As they emerged from the cave and stepped back into the sunlight, Emma felt the pendant vibrate, as if urging them onward. They still had a fight ahead of them, and with the Heart of the Village in their hearts, they were ready to face whatever challenges lay ahead.

CHAPTER 11

THE RETURN OF BALTHAZAR

The sun hung high in the sky as the friends made their way back to the village, their hearts pounding with a mix of excitement and apprehension. With the Heart of the Village resonating within them, they knew they had to prepare for the confrontation with Balthazar.

As they approached the village square, they were met by the concerned faces of the villagers. Whispers filled the air, and a sense of unease hung over them like a thick fog.

Emma, sensing their worry, quickened her pace to reach Thaddeus's workshop. Inside, Thaddeus was examining the sundial, his brow furrowed with concentration. When he noticed the trio entering, his expression shifted from worry to relief. "You've returned! Did you find the Heart?" "Yes, and we learned so much!" Zoe exclaimed, unable to contain her excitement. "But Balthazar is coming. We have to protect the sundial!" Thaddeus nodded gravely, his hands tightening around the sundial's edge. "I feared he wouldn't stay away for long. He has his sights set on the sundial's power, and he won't rest until he gets it." Emma felt a surge of determination. "We can't let him win.

We have the Heart, and we know its power now. We need to rally the villagers and prepare for his arrival." With Thaddeus's guidance, the friends quickly gathered the villagers in the square, explaining the importance of the sundial and the Heart of the Village. They urged everyone to remain vigilant and to come together as a community.

As the sun began to set, casting a golden glow over the village, Emma couldn't shake the feeling that time was running out. She stood at the front, her heart pounding as she addressed the crowd. "We are the guardians of this village now, and we must protect what is ours. Together, we can face whatever challenges come our way!" The villagers nodded, their faces set with resolve.

Just then, a chill swept through the air, and the sky darkened as storm clouds rolled in. Emma felt a shiver run down her spine. "It's him," she whispered, her eyes scanning the horizon.

As if summoned by her words, Balthazar appeared, silhouetted against the darkening sky. His presence sent a wave of fear rippling through the crowd, but Emma stood her ground, the warmth of the Heart filling her with courage. "Children," Balthazar called out, his voice dripping with disdain, "do you really believe you can stop me? The sundial belongs to me! Hand it over, and I may spare you."

Emma stepped forward, her heart racing. "The sundial is not yours to take! It's a part of our village, our history, and we will protect it." Balthazar laughed, a cold, chilling sound that echoed through the square. "You think you can defy me? I know the secrets of the sundial far better than you do. You're merely children playing at being heroes." With a flick of his wrist, dark shadows swirled around him, and the air crackled with ominous energy. Emma felt a rush of fear but quickly remembered the warmth of the Heart within her. "We have the Heart of the Village!" Zoe shouted, holding her ground beside Emma. "We will protect it, no matter what!" Balthazar's expression shifted, a flicker of concern crossing his face.

"The Heart? You've found it? That's a mistake you'll regret!" With a roar, he unleashed a torrent of dark energy towards them. Emma, instinctively raising her hands, felt the Heart resonate within her. "Now!" she shouted. The three friends joined hands, and as they focused on the Heart's power, a barrier of light enveloped them, pushing back against Balthazar's dark magic.

The villagers gasped, watching in awe as the clash of energies filled the square with brilliant colors. "Your darkness cannot overcome the light of our village!" Emma cried, her voice rising above the chaos. "Together, we are stronger!" With a surge of determination, they pushed against Balthazar's magic, channeling the strength of the villagers around them. The barrier grew brighter, pushing back the darkness and forcing Balthazar to stagger back. "You think you can win?!" he shouted, anger boiling in his voice. "I will have what is mine!" As Balthazar unleashed another wave of energy, Emma felt the Heart guiding her thoughts.

"We have to show him that the power of the sundial belongs to the village, not to him!" Drawing on the energy of the villagers, Emma envisioned the sundial as a beacon of hope, a symbol of unity. "We are the protectors of time! We will not let you destroy our past or our future!" The light from the Heart flared, enveloping the entire square. The villagers stood united, their voices rising in a chorus of support. The combined energy was overwhelming, creating a surge that pushed Balthazar back further. Realizing he was losing ground, Balthazar's eyes narrowed in fury. "This isn't over!" he hissed, before vanishing into the shadows with a final burst of dark energy. The villagers erupted in cheers as the darkness dissipated, replaced by the warm glow of the setting sun. Emma, Liam, and Zoe stood in a protective circle around the sundial, their hearts racing with adrenaline and triumph. Thaddeus stepped forward, his face filled with pride. "You did it! You defended the sundial and the village!" Emma looked around at her friends and the villagers, a wave of joy washing over her. "We did it together! The Heart of the Village gave us the strength we needed."

As the villagers celebrated their victory, Emma felt a sense of purpose solidifying within her. But even as they reveled in their success, she couldn't shake the feeling that Balthazar would return. They had won this battle, but the war for the sundial's protection was far from over. "Let's prepare for what's next," Liam said, breaking her thoughts. "We need to be ready in case Balthazar tries again." Emma nodded, determination rekindled in her heart.

They would not back down. With the Heart of the Village guiding them, they were ready to face whatever challenges lay ahead. But as the stars began to twinkle in the night sky, Emma felt the weight of their journey pressing down on her. There was still so much to learn, and the mysteries of time awaited them.

CHAPTER 12

A NEW DAWN

The celebration in the village square continued long into the night. Lanterns lit up the space, casting a warm glow over the joyful faces of the villagers. Emma, Liam, and Zoe stood together, sharing smiles of relief and triumph.

Thaddeus gathered everyone around the sundial, now shimmering with the soft light of the Heart. "Let this sundial be a reminder of our unity and strength. We have faced darkness and emerged victorious," he declared, his voice resonating with pride.

The villagers cheered, raising their hands in solidarity. Emma felt a swell of emotion. They had come together as a community, and that bond had given them the power to protect what was dear to them. As the festivities continued, Emma's thoughts drifted. "We've won this battle," she said quietly to Liam and Zoe, "but Balthazar will come back.

We need to be ready for whatever he throws at us next." Liam nodded, his expression serious. "He won't give up easily. We've seen his determination, and he's powerful. We have to learn everything we can about the sundial and the Heart." Zoe chimed in, "And we should gather more allies.

There may be others who can help us understand the magic of the sundial and the history of our village." Just then, the village elder approached them, her silver hair glistening in the lantern light. "You three have shown great bravery," she said, her voice warm and wise. "The village has not seen protectors like you in many years. Your journey has just begun."

Emma felt a sense of responsibility settle on her shoulders. "We want to protect the village and the sundial. We want to learn everything about our history and how we can continue to defend it." The elder smiled, her eyes twinkling. "Then it is time for you to explore the depths of your heritage. There are many stories yet untold, and they hold the key to understanding your roles as guardians."

As the elder spoke, Emma's mind raced with possibilities. They could delve into the lore of the village, uncovering forgotten tales and hidden truths that would prepare them for the challenges ahead. "We can start tomorrow!" Zoe exclaimed, her excitement contagious. "We can explore the library and visit the elder's archives. There must be records of past guardians and their battles." "Exactly," Liam said, a determined look on his face. "We'll learn what we need to know to stay one step ahead of Balthazar."

As the night wore on, Emma took a moment to step away from the festivities and gaze up at the stars. The moon shone brightly, illuminating the village and the sundial that had become the heart of their community. She felt the weight of the Heart of the Village still lingering within her, a constant reminder of their purpose. Just then, she felt a soft tap on her shoulder.

Turning, she found Thaddeus beside her. "Emma, I wanted to speak with you." "What is it?" she asked, curious. "The Heart of the Village chose you for a reason," he said, his voice low and serious. "You have the potential to be a great leader. Trust in yourself and your instincts, and you will find your way."

Emma felt a warmth spread through her, bolstered by Thaddeus's words. "Thank you, Thaddeus. I want to be the best guardian I can be, for the village and for my friends." He nodded. "And remember, you're not alone. You have Liam and Zoe by your side, and the village stands with you. Together, you can face any challenge."

As the celebrations began to wind down, Emma joined her friends once more, their faces alight with enthusiasm as they shared ideas for their next steps.

"Let's make a plan," Liam said, spreading out the old map of the village they had found in the library. "We can mark the locations of significant historical sites. Maybe we'll discover more about the timekeepers and the magic that surrounds us." Zoe nodded, pulling out her notebook. "I'll start jotting down everything we've learned so far and our ideas for what to investigate next." Emma looked at her friends, feeling grateful for their camaraderie. "I couldn't ask for better friends to embark on this journey with.

We'll make sure the village is safe, and we'll uncover all the mysteries waiting for us." As the first light of dawn began to break over the horizon, Emma felt a renewed sense of hope.

The adventure of a lifetime awaited them, filled with history, secrets, and the promise of more time-traveling escapades. With the Heart of the Village guiding their way, they were ready to face whatever lay ahead, united as guardians of time.

And somewhere in the shadows, Balthazar watched, plotting his next move. The game was far from over.

NEXT TITLE

THE PHARAOH'S PUZZLE

BOOK 2

After their thrilling adventure in the medieval village, Emma, Liam, and Zoe return home, but they can't shake the feeling that Balthazar's threat still lingers.

When they find mysterious hieroglyphs appearing on the sundial, they're pulled back in time to ancient Egypt, a world of towering pyramids, hidden tombs, and an empire ruled by the young Pharaoh Akhenaten.

The trio must solve a cryptic puzzle hidden deep within the Pharaoh's palace, a secret code that holds the key to an ancient treasure capable of shifting the course of Egyptian history.

But they aren't the only ones on the hunt. Balthazar has followed them, determined to claim the treasure's power for himself.

As Emma, Liam, and Zoe decode hieroglyphs, navigate treacherous sand dunes, and befriend a clever Egyptian scribe, they learn just how high the stakes have become.

With every step, they come closer to unraveling the Pharaoh's secret, but they also come closer to facing Balthazar in a race against time.

Will they unlock the puzzle before it's too late? Or will they lose the game and risk being trapped in ancient Egypt forever?